min_edition

published by Penguin Young Readers Group

Illustrations copyright © 2007 by Claudia Carls

Original title: Von dem Breikesssel, 1854 in "Märchen und Sagen aus Hannover.

English text adaption by Anthea Bell

Coproduction with Michael Neugebauer Publishing Ltd., Hong Kong.

Rights arranged with "minedition" Rights and Licensing AG, Zurich, Switzerland.

Published simultaneously in Canada.

Manufactured in China by Wide World Ltd.

Typesetting in Silentium Pro by Jovica Veljovic

Color separation and computer graphics by the artist

Library of Congress Cataloging-in-Publication Data available upon request.

ISBN 978-0-698-40073-3

1846

10 9 8 7 6 5 4 3 2 1

First Impression

For more information please visit our website:
www.minedition.com

The Porridge Pot

1854 by the Brothers Carl and Theodor Colshorn

retold from the German by Anthea Bell

with pictures by Claudia Carls

minedition

Once upon a time, seven miles beyond Cloud-Cuckoo-Land, there lived a man and a woman, and they were always eating and drinking and making merry. The man was a miller, the woman was his wife, and they had an only daughter. The girl was so beautiful that when she sat by the millstream in summer, washing her feet, all the fish swam up and jumped out of the water for joy.

But then hard times came, not much grain was brought to the mill for grinding, and so the miller and his family had no money to buy food. One day the miller's wife tipped the last remains out of all the kitchen jars she had, knocked what little flour was left out of the empty bags, added the last of their salt, and made rye porridge. "This will be our last meal," she said, "and when we've eaten it we might as well lie down and die."

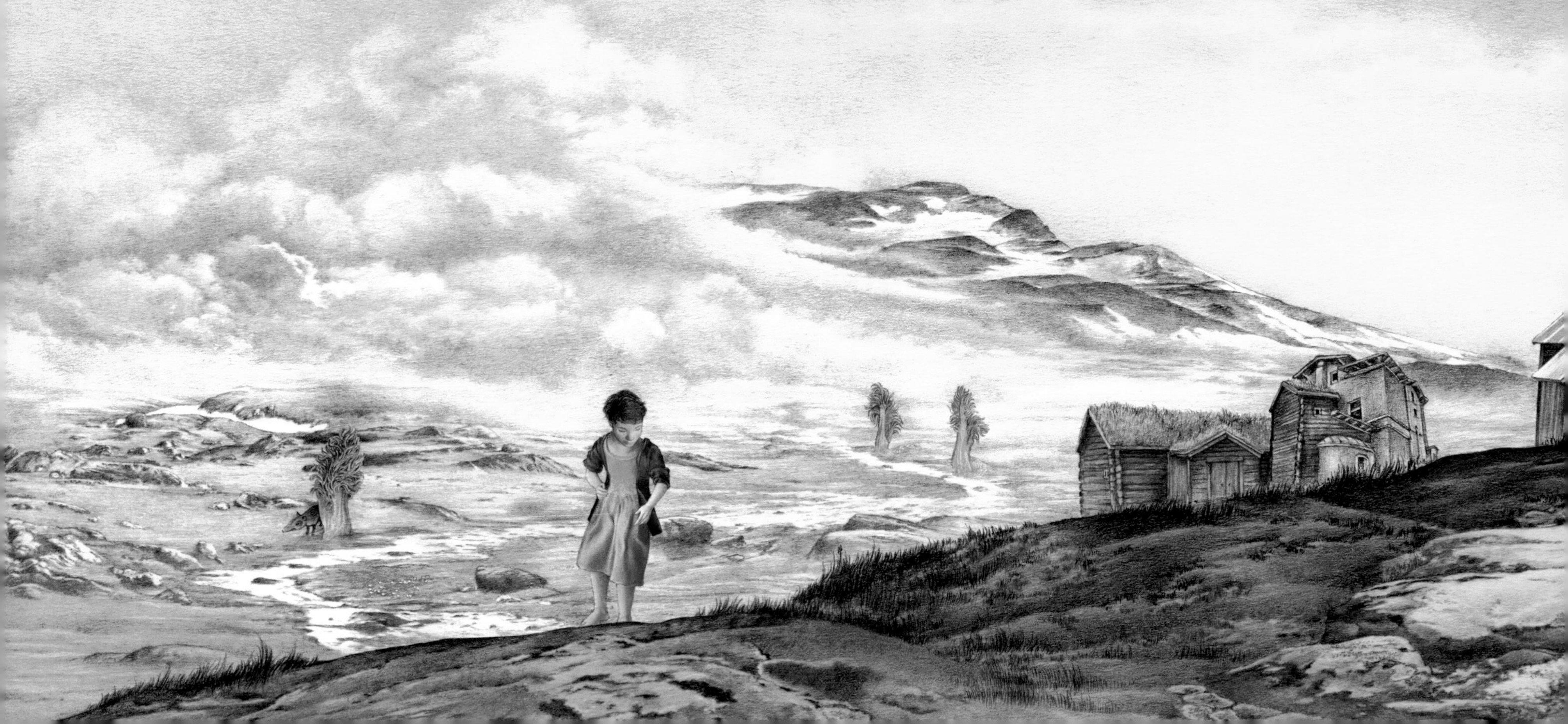

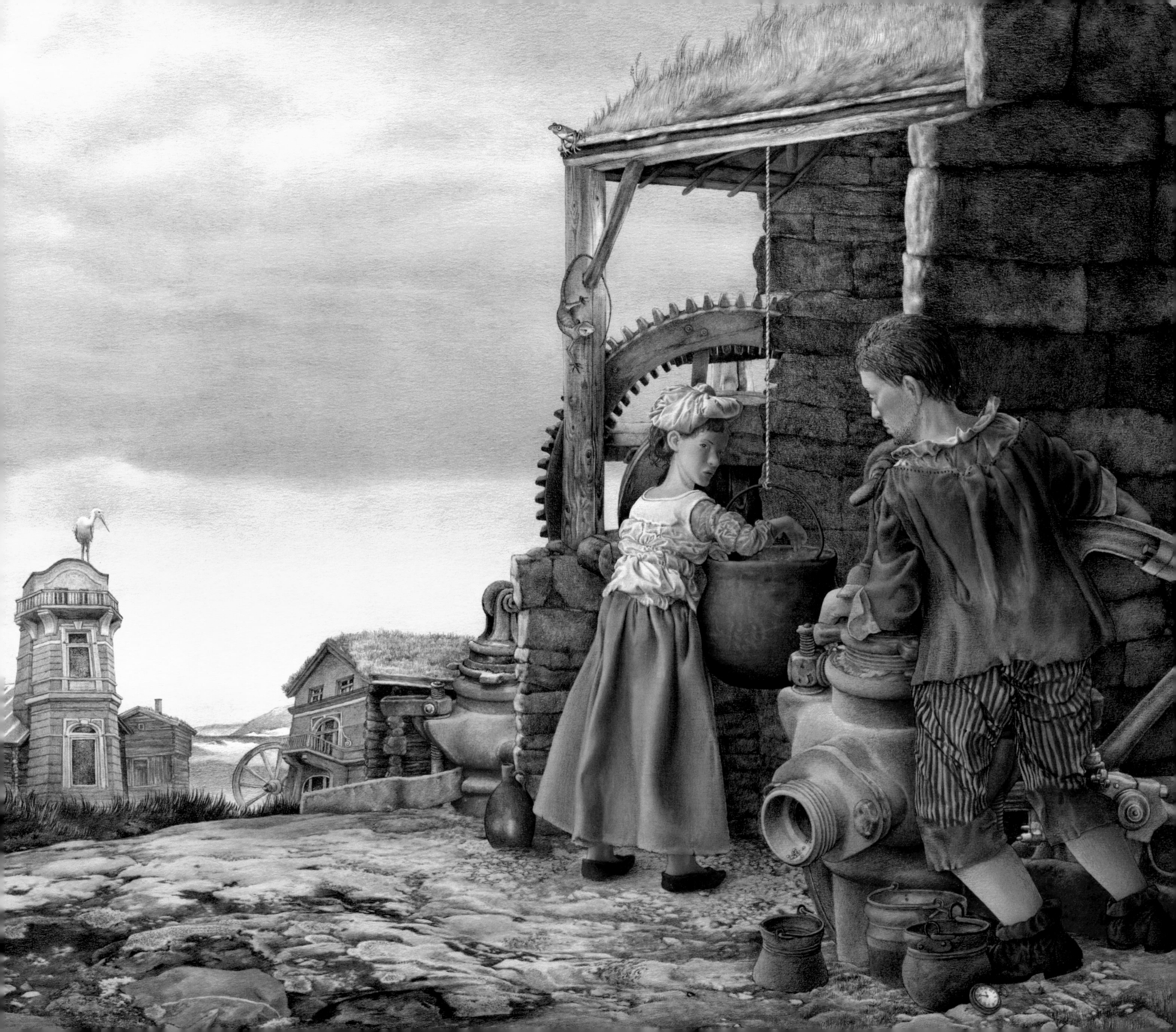

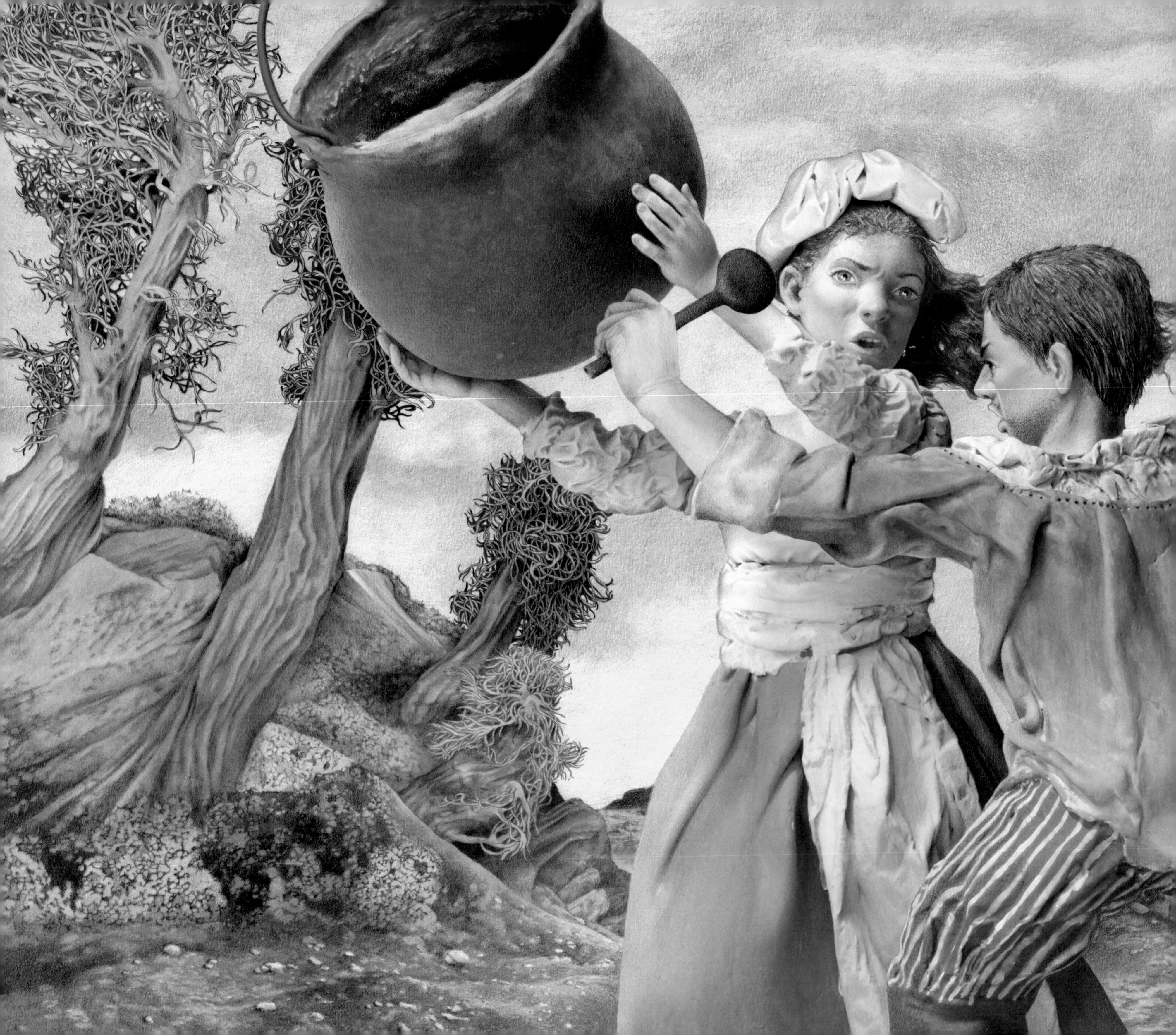

When the porridge was ready, the miller came into the kitchen and picked up a wooden spoon to taste it. But his wife wouldn't let him, and when she saw that he was determined to take a spoonful she put the pot on her head and ran away, with her hair flying loose. The man ran after her, still with the spoon in his hand, and when their daughter saw them go she picked up her shoes and followed her father.

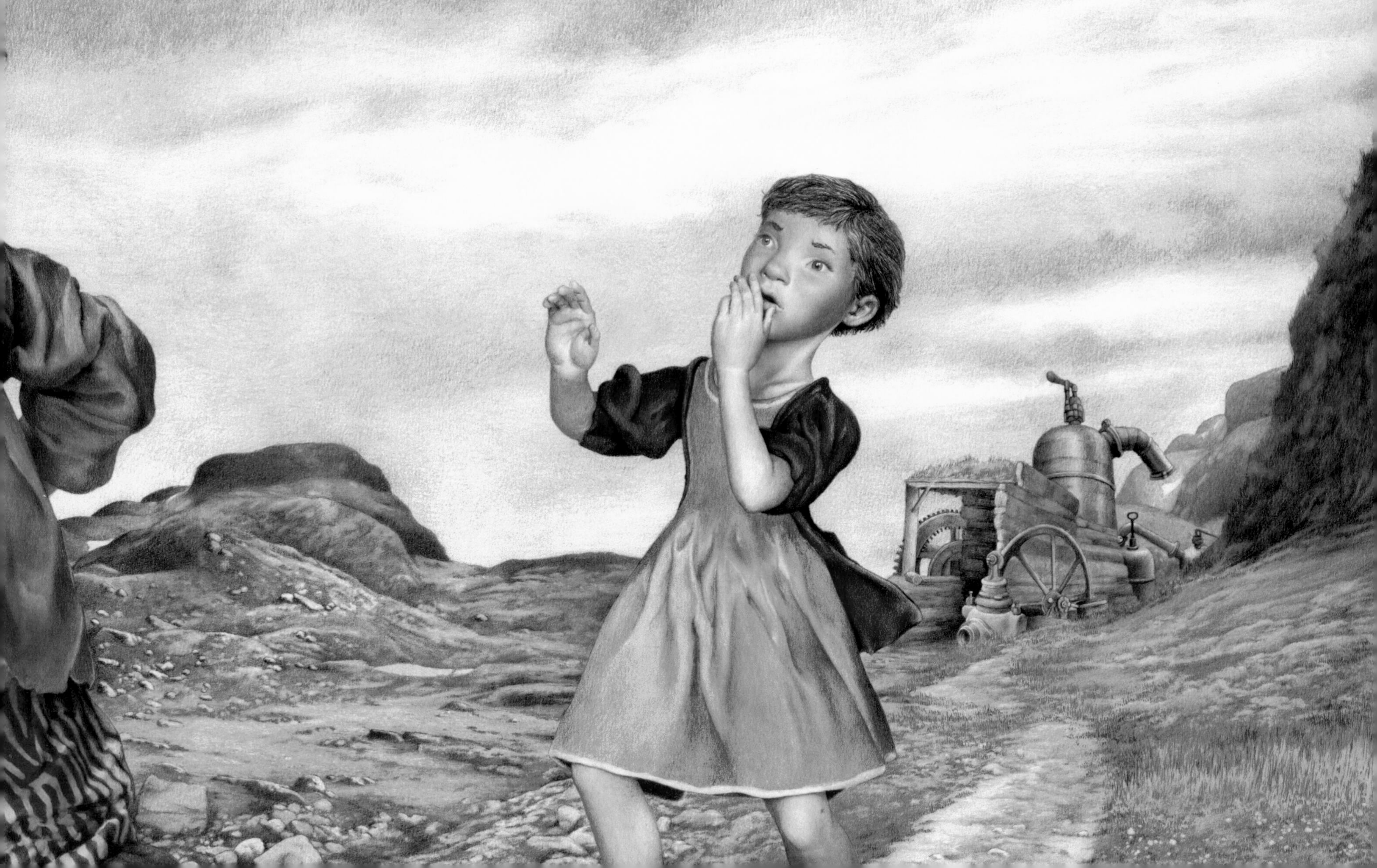

Well, they came to a forest, where the girl lost one of her shoes, and while she was looking for it her mother and father disappeared among the trees. Then she sat down behind a bush, because she was so tired that she could go no farther, and she wept and wailed. And when she remembered that she'd lost one of her shoes she wept even more. As for the shoe, the wren had found it, and his wife Jenny Wren was using it as a cradle and rocking her babies in it.

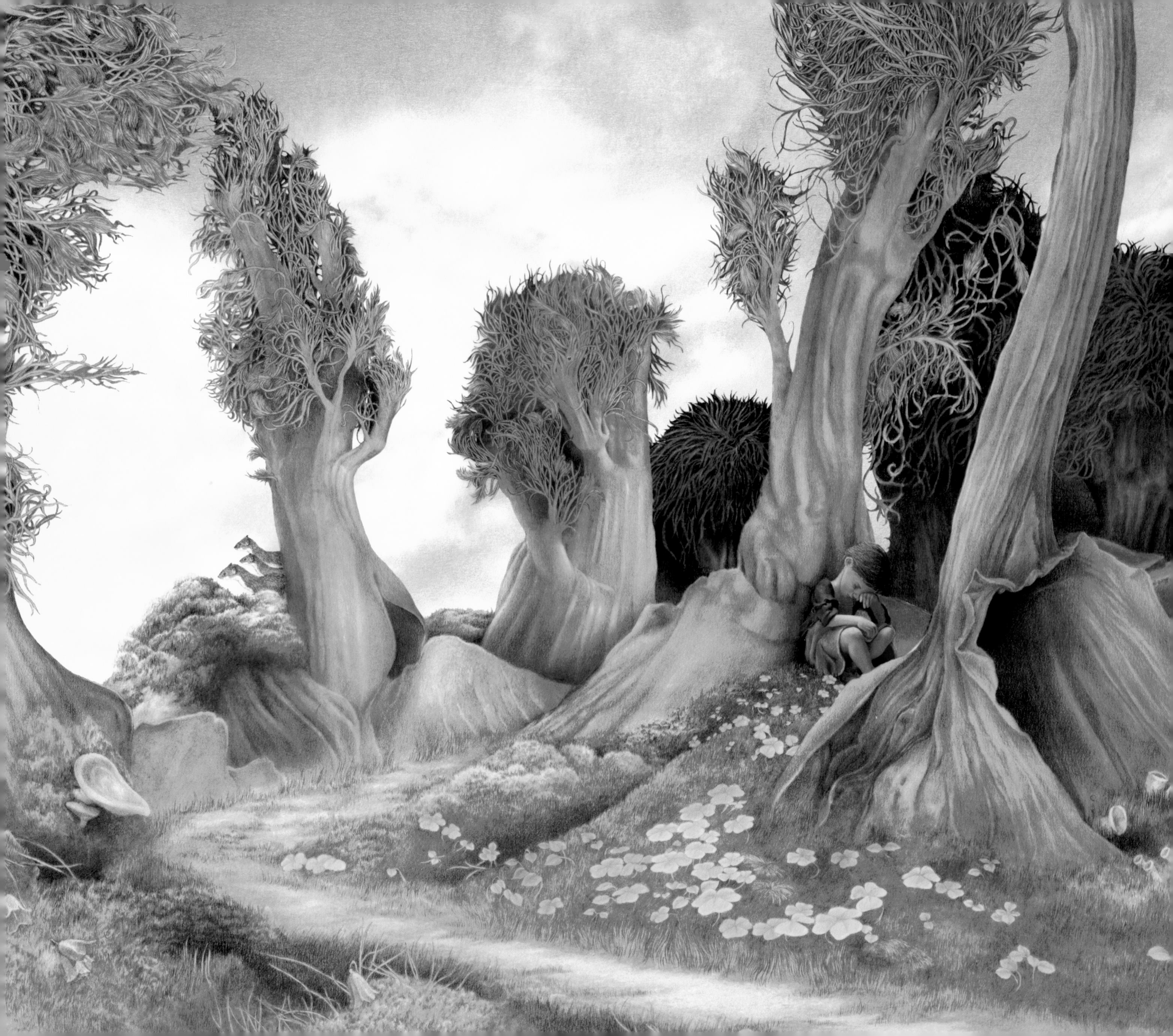

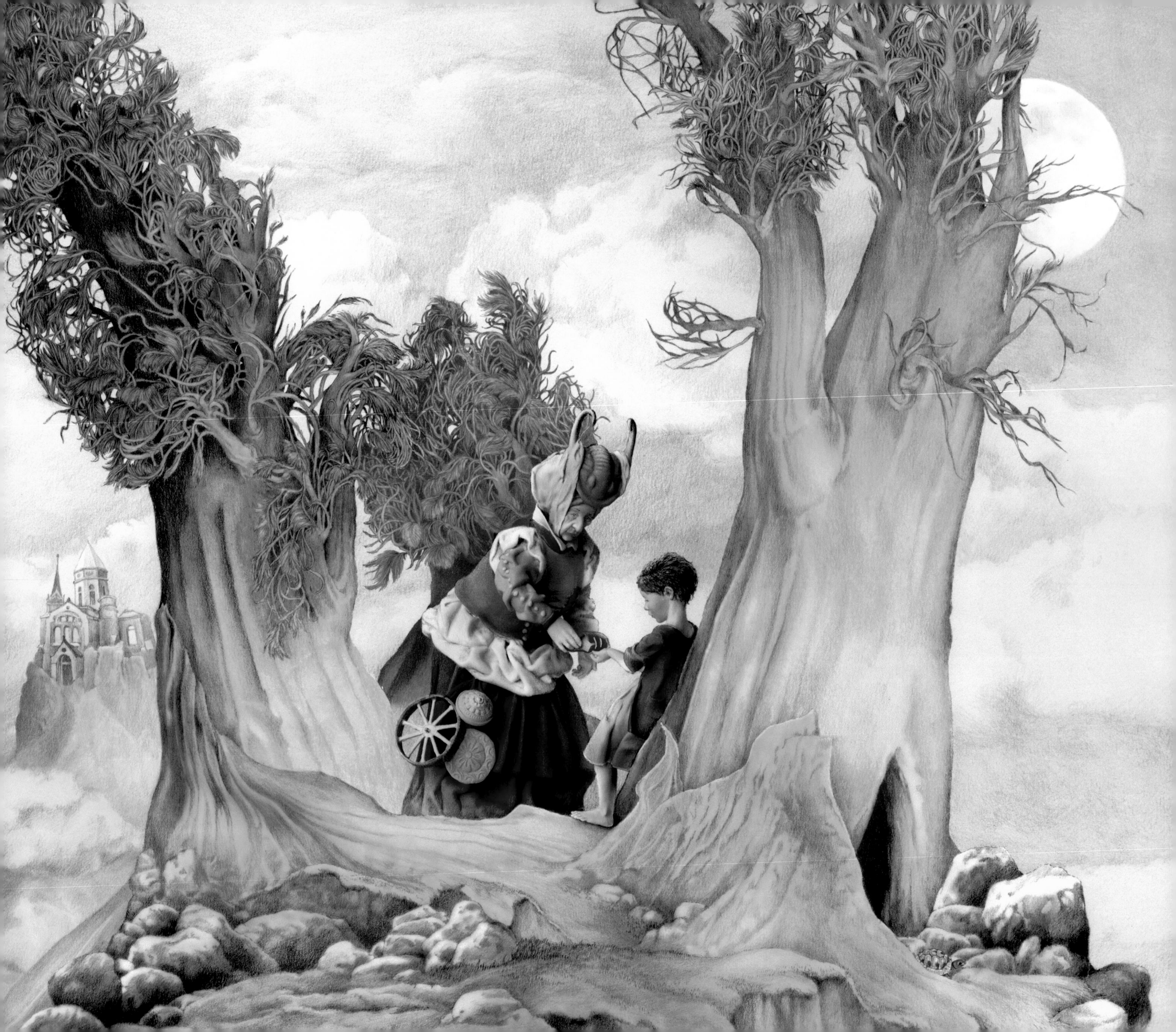

As the girl sat there, lamenting pitifully enough to soften a heart of stone, she suddenly saw an old woman standing beside her. "What's the matter, my child?" asked the old woman. So the girl replied, "My mother made porridge with the very last of our flour, and my father wanted to taste it, but my mother wouldn't let him. Now she's run away with the porridge pot on her head, and my father is running after her with a spoon in his hand. And when I went after them myself I lost a shoe, and while I was looking for it my mother and father disappeared among the trees. What am I to do now? Oh, if only I had my shoe back!"

"Here's another for you," said the old woman, bringing a brand-new shoe out of her bag, and she added, "Now stop crying, do as I tell you, and all will be well! Go a little farther into the forest and you'll come to a large house. It's a royal palace, and you must go in. When they show you a great many dresses made of silk, cotton, or linen, and they tell you to choose one, pick out the very best silk dress you can see, and when they ask you why you choose that one, you must reply, 'I was brought up to wear silk.'"

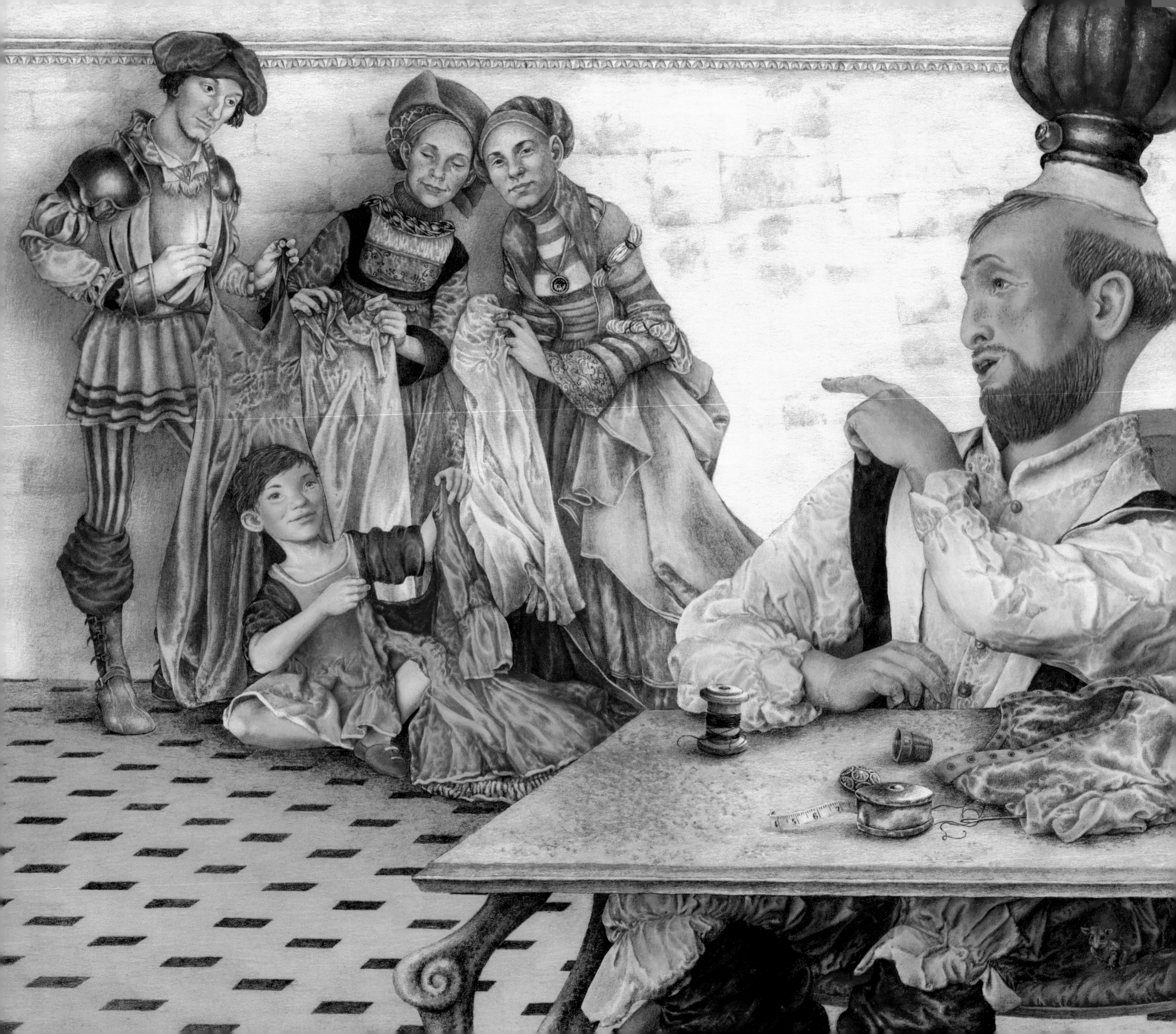

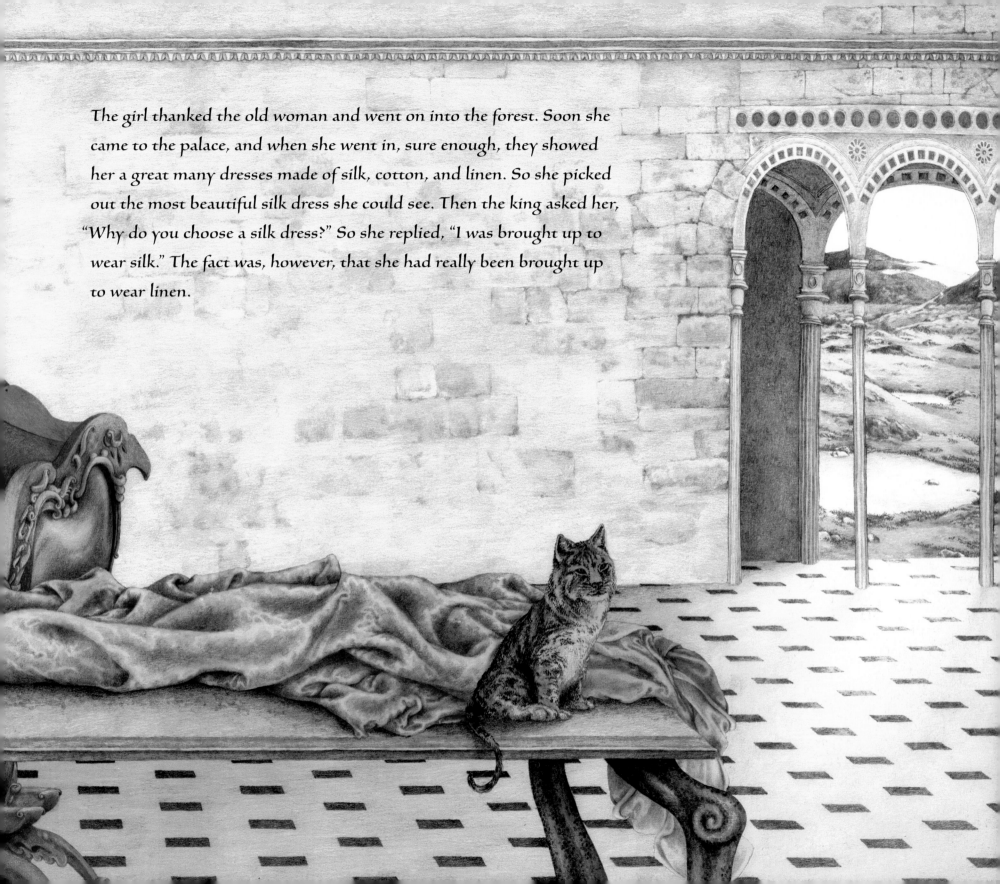

The girl thanked the old woman and went on into the forest. Soon she came to the palace, and when she went in, sure enough, they showed her a great many dresses made of silk, cotton, and linen. So she picked out the most beautiful silk dress she could see. Then the king asked her, "Why do you choose a silk dress?" So she replied, "I was brought up to wear silk." The fact was, however, that she had really been brought up to wear linen.

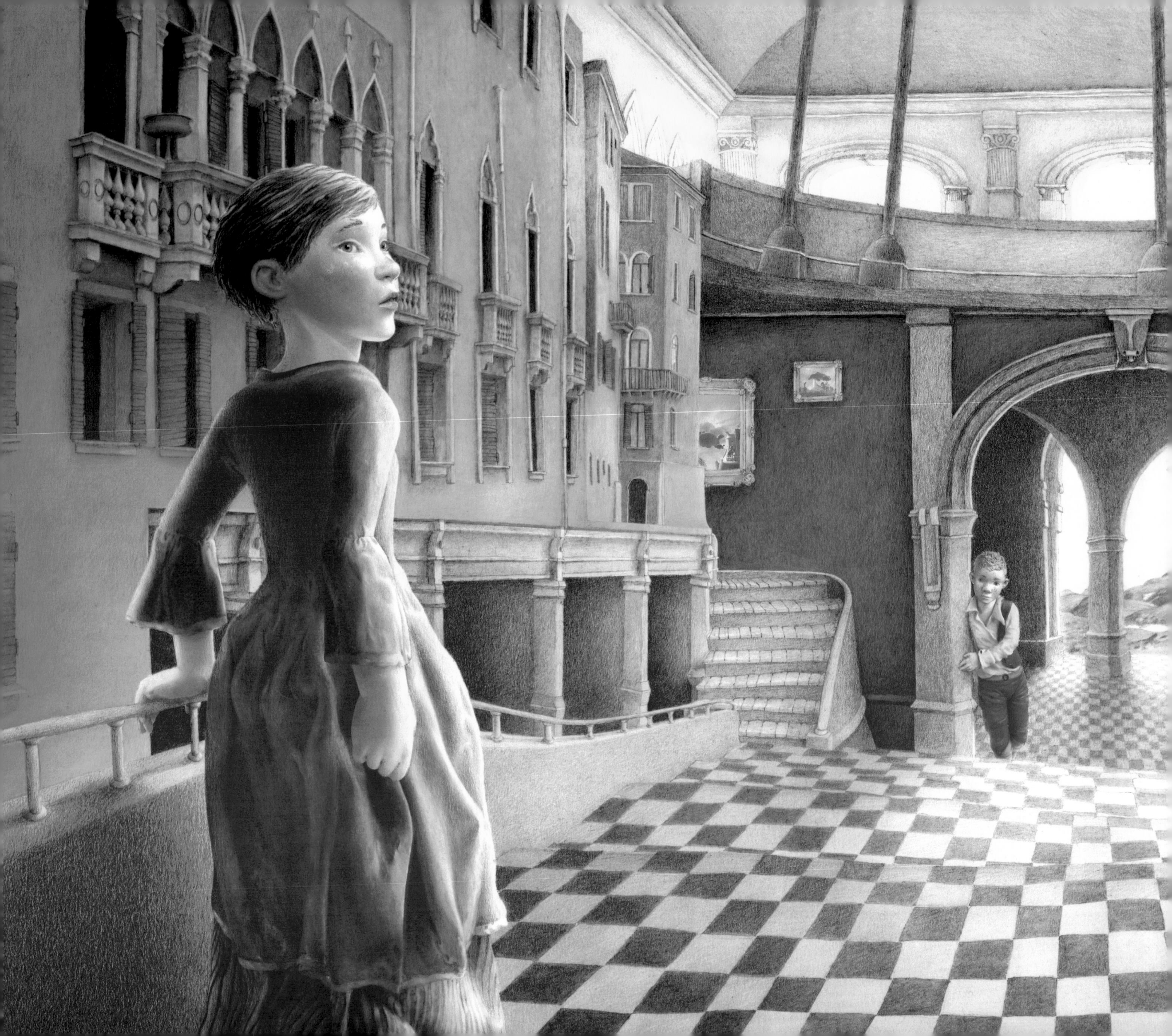

Well, the king had a son, a prince who was twelve years old, and now he was to get married. When the miller's daughter came in wearing the silk dress his heart warmed to her, and he said, "Dear Father, if I must really be married then give me this girl for my wife, for I will never marry anyone else!" Then they were all glad, and the wedding day was fixed.

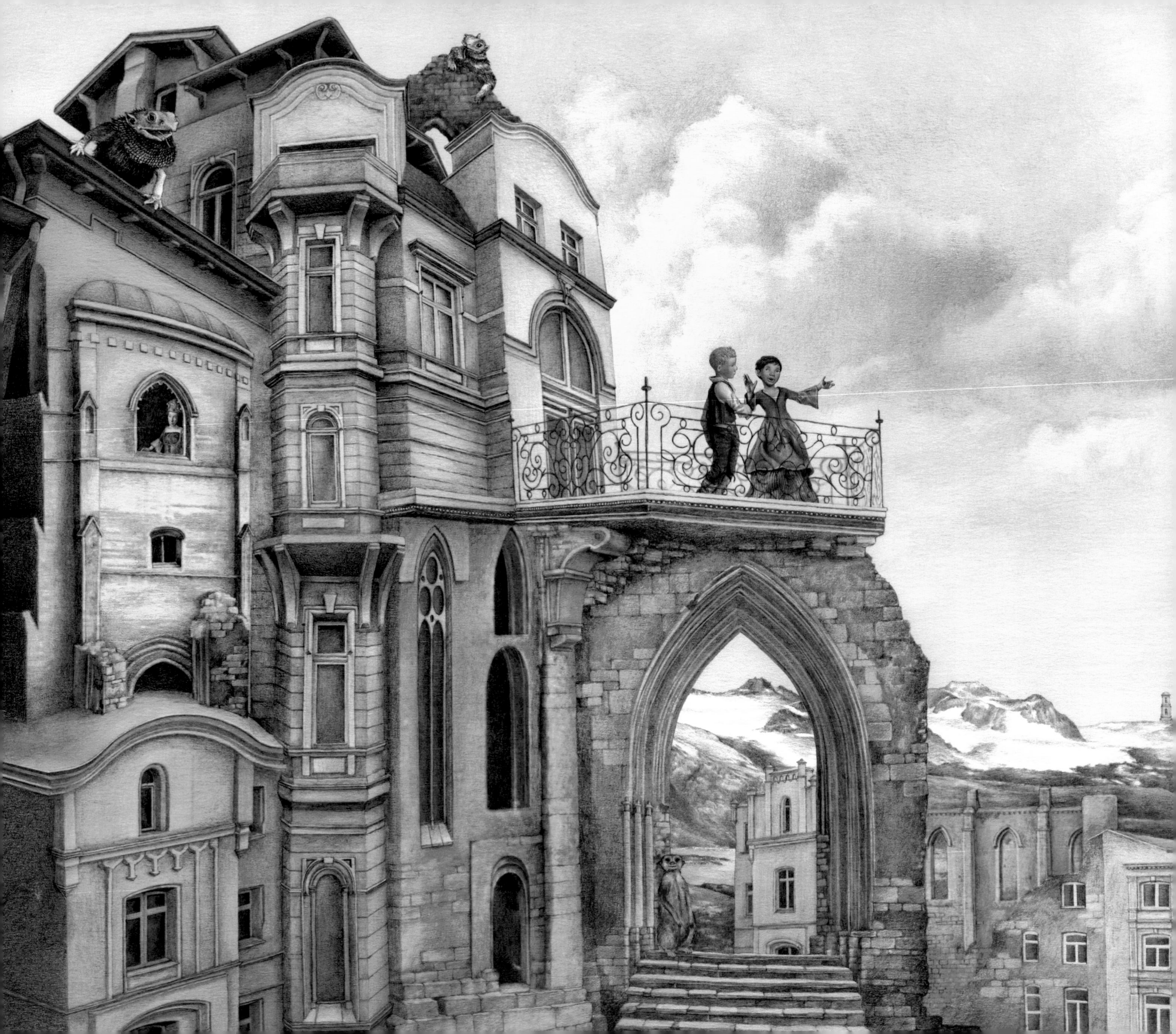

One day the young bride was standing upstairs on the balcony outside the great hall of the palace, looking down. Then she saw her mother running past with the porridge pot on her head and her hair flying loose, and behind her came the girl's father with the big wooden spoon in his hand. At that she had to laugh out loud; she couldn't help it.

The prince, who was in the next room, heard her. He came in and said, "What are you laughing at, dearest?" She didn't want to tell the story of her parents, so she replied, "I was laughing at the idea of being married in this little palace. Where will we ever find room for all the guests?" And the prince replied, "Why, do you have a larger palace?" "Yes, much larger," she said. But really she didn't have any palace at all. "Oh," said the prince, "then let's put the wedding off for a week! We'll invite all the guests to your palace, we'll drive over and hold the wedding there." And with these words he went away to tell his father.

But as for the girl, she went down into the courtyard feeling very sad, for how was she to come by a large palace? And as she sat weeping and wailing, there was the old woman beside her again all of a sudden. "What's the matter?" she asked. "Oh," said the girl, "when I was standing on the balcony outside the great hall of the palace, looking down, I saw my parents running past and I couldn't help laughing out loud. My bridegroom, who was in the next room, heard me, and when he came and asked why I was laughing I pretended it was because this is such a little palace, and I said I had a much larger one. Now they want to hold the wedding there, but I don't have any palace at all."

"Yes, you do!" replied the old woman. "Just stop crying, drive off with your bridegroom in a carriage, and when you've been driving a little way a white poodle will jump out of the bushes. No one but you will be able to see it. Wherever the poodle goes, have your carriage driven after it." With these words the old woman disappeared and the girl went back to the great hall.

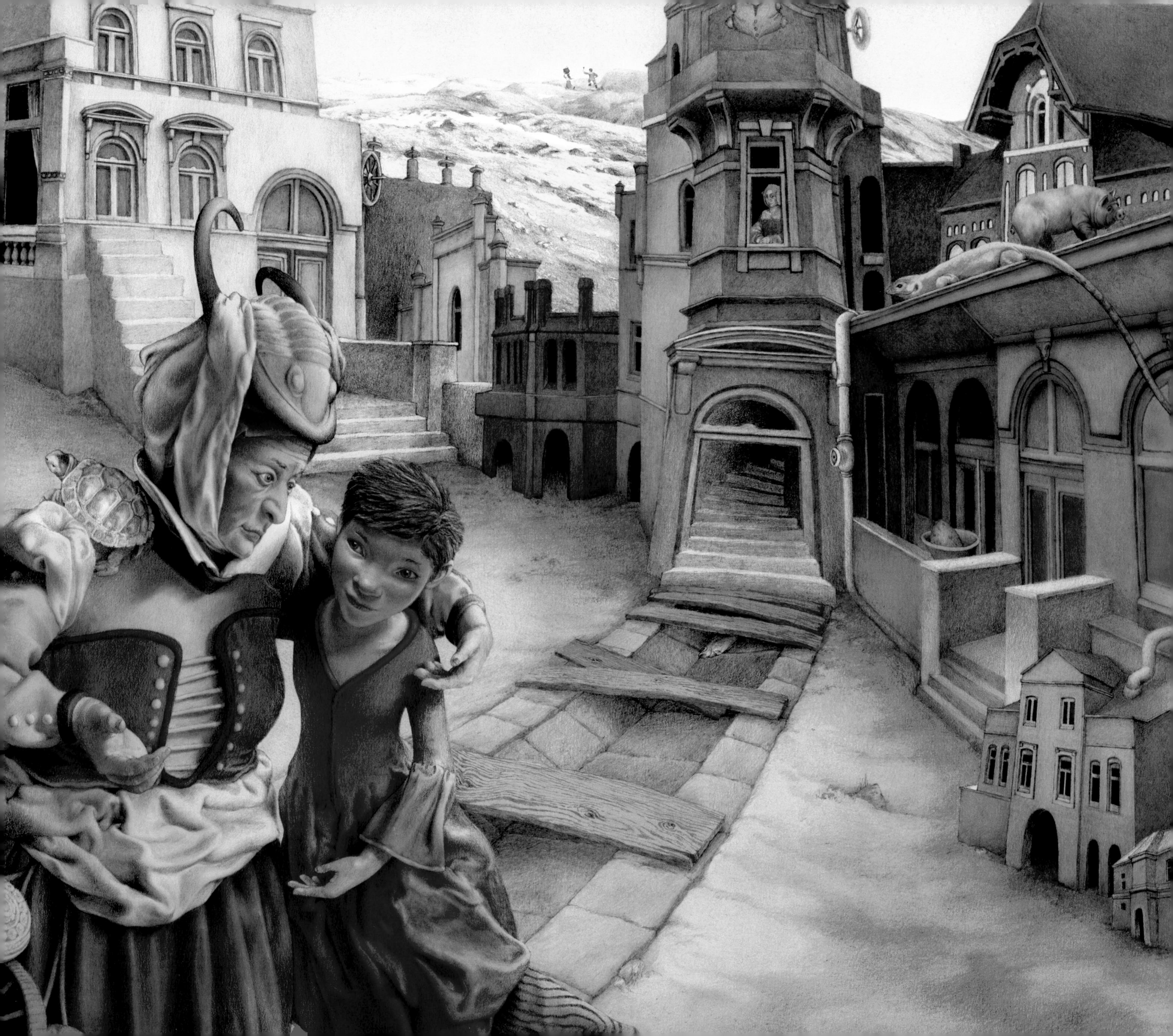

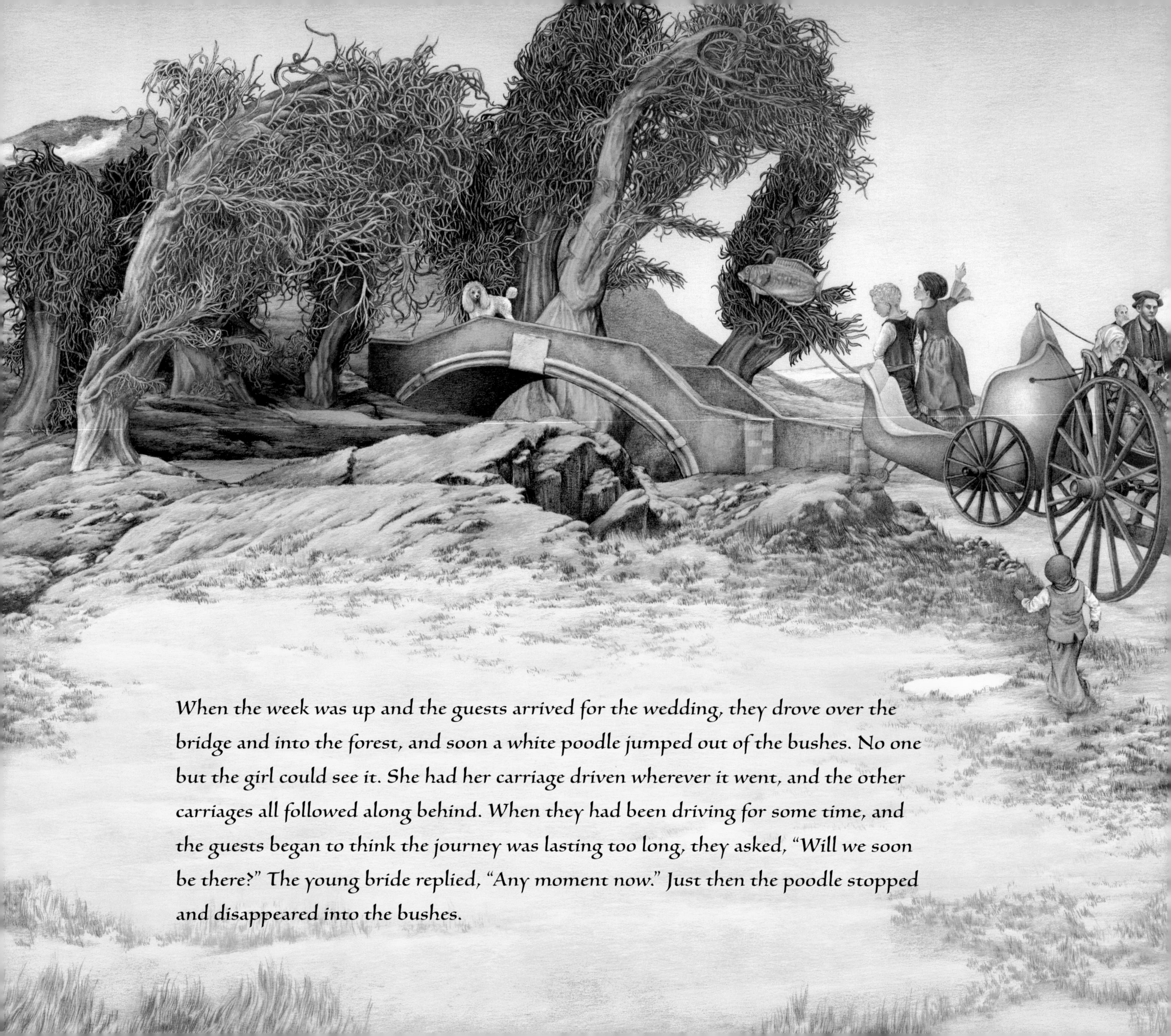

When the week was up and the guests arrived for the wedding, they drove over the bridge and into the forest, and soon a white poodle jumped out of the bushes. No one but the girl could see it. She had her carriage driven wherever it went, and the other carriages all followed along behind. When they had been driving for some time, and the guests began to think the journey was lasting too long, they asked, "Will we soon be there?" The young bride replied, "Any moment now." Just then the poodle stopped and disappeared into the bushes.

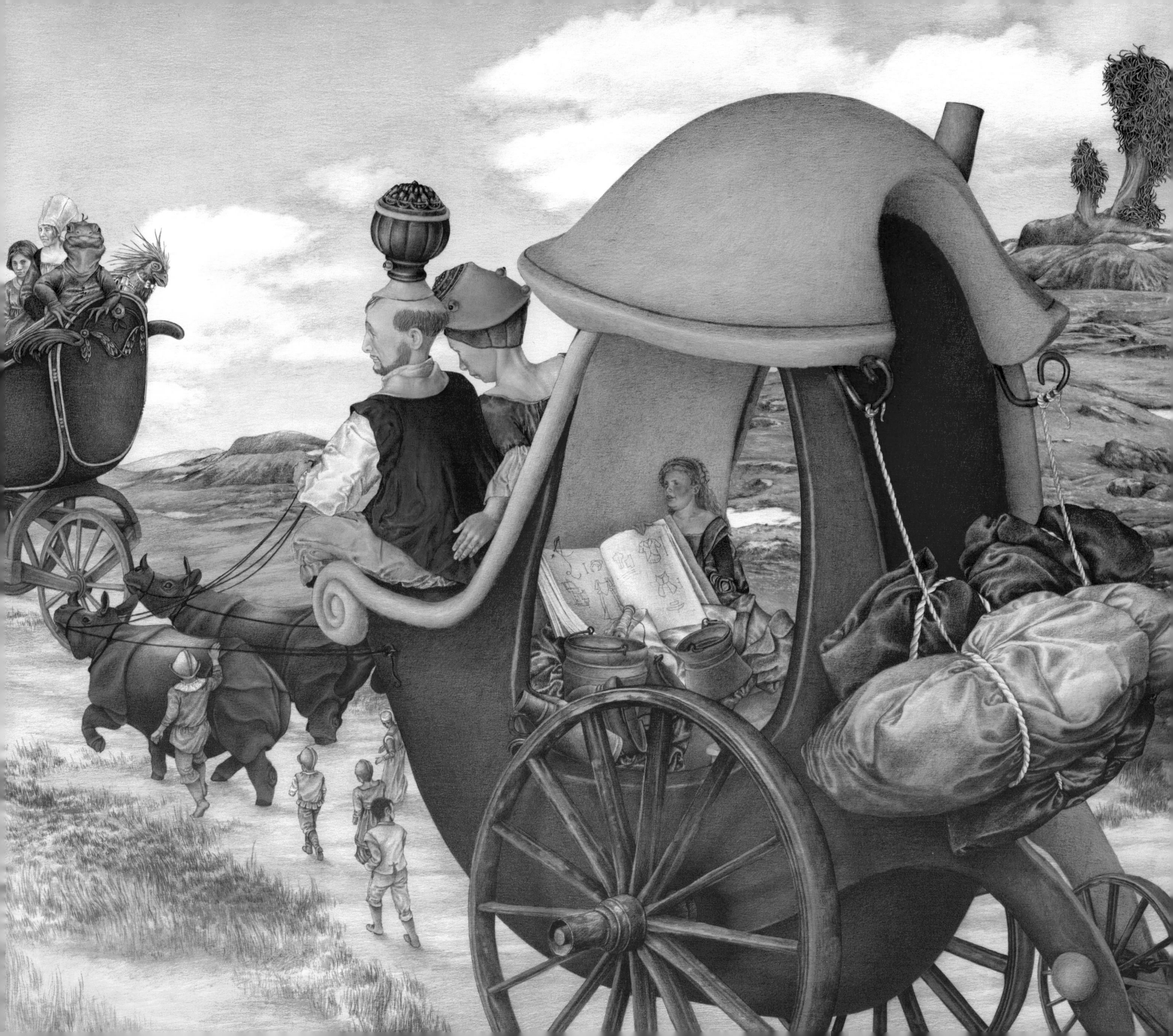

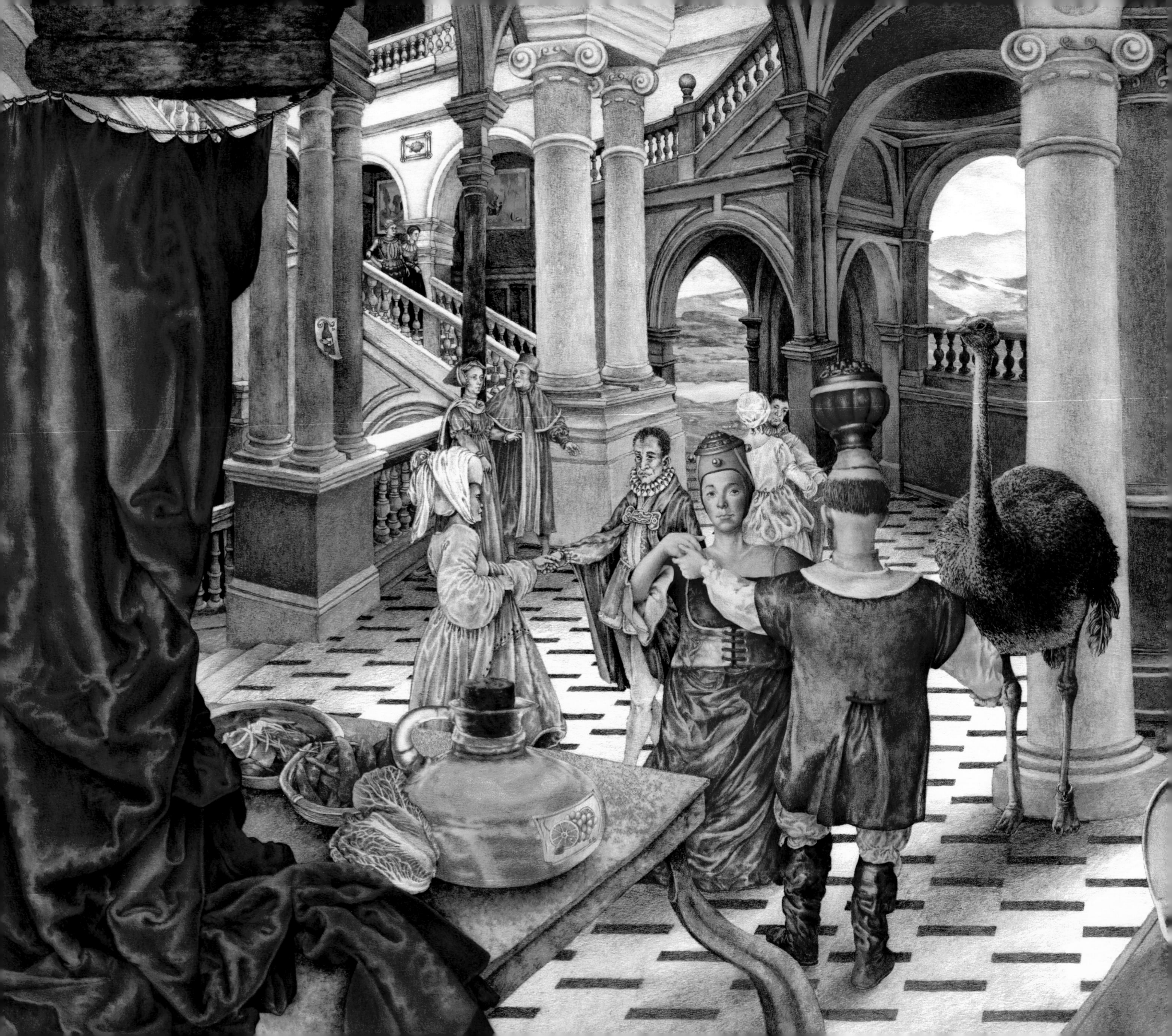

And suddenly, just where the poodle had disappeared, they all saw a large palace with tall towers, bright windows, and smoke rising from the chimney-pots. "This is my palace," said the bride, and they climbed out of their carriages and went in. And what do you think? – tables were laid, beds were made up, and servants were running in and out. So the young couple were married, and the wedding festivities went on for six months.

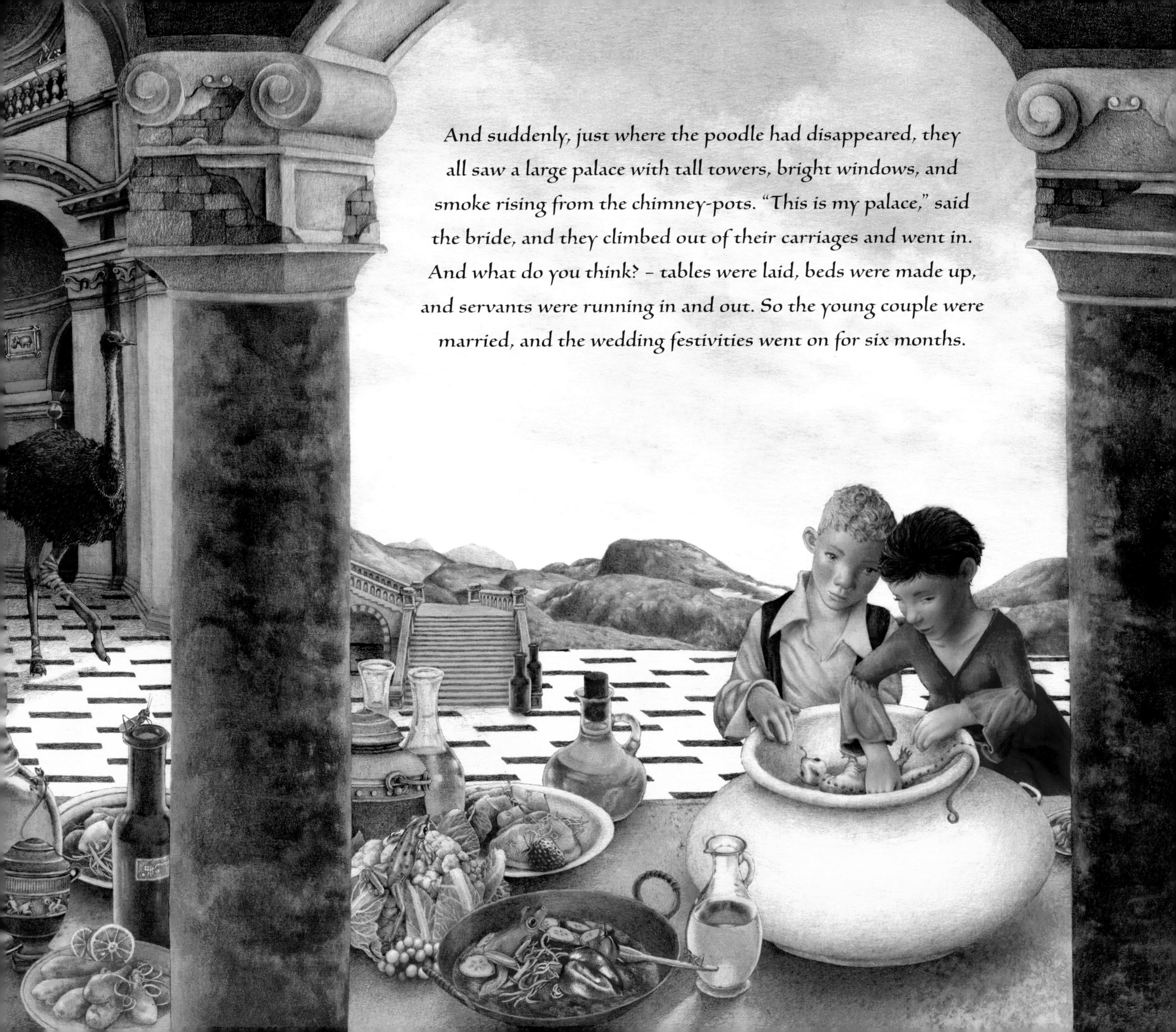

On the last day of the festivities, when everything was packed up ready to go back to the old palace and they were sitting for dinner in the larger one for the last time, something suddenly collided with the door, which flew open with a crash. "My lady the queen! My lady the queen!" cried a woman who came running in with a porridge pot on her head. "Protect me, my lady the queen! My husband is going to beat me!"

And then her husband came in too with a wooden spoon, in a furious temper. But when he saw all those grand guests, he stopped.

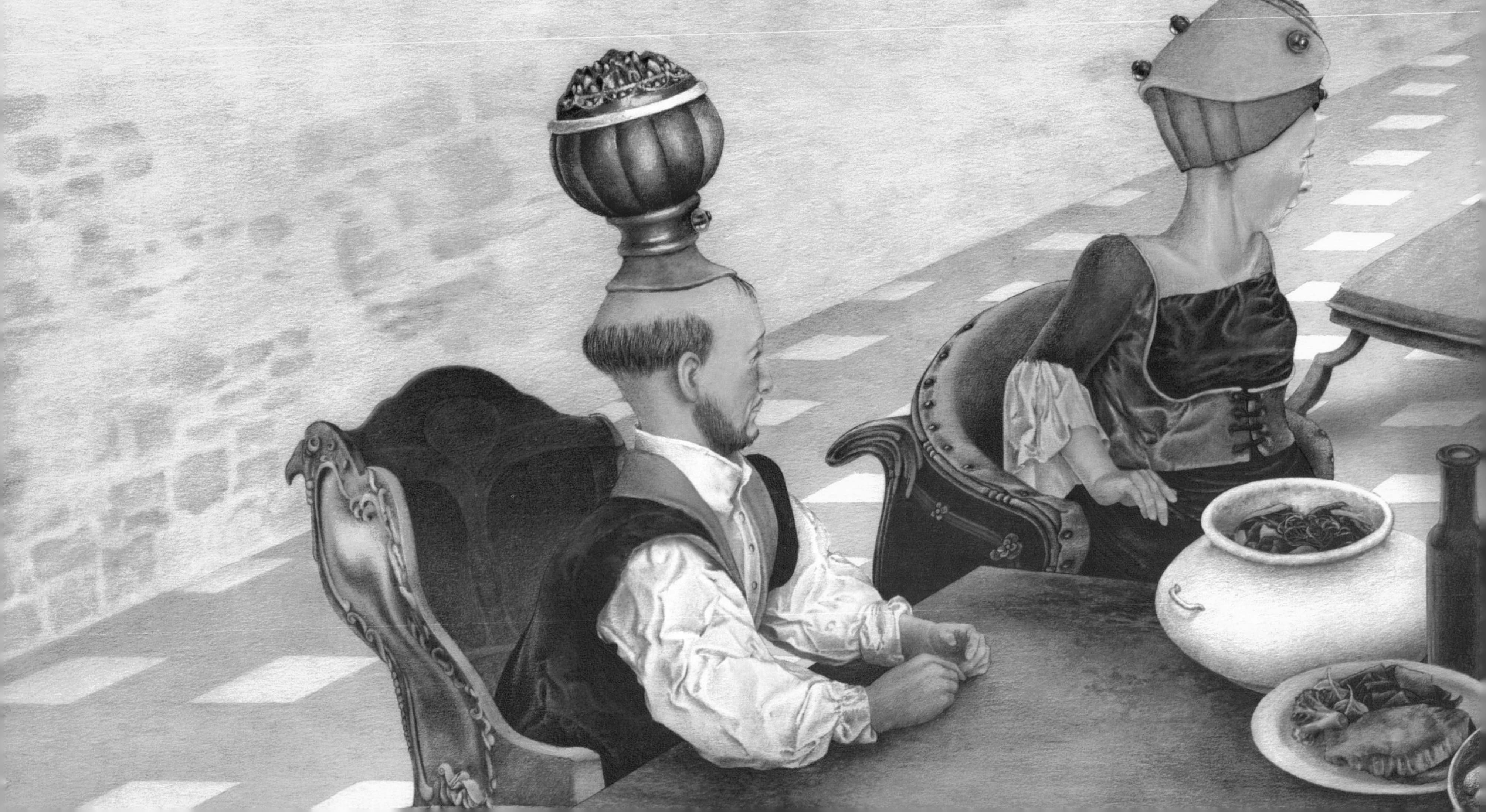

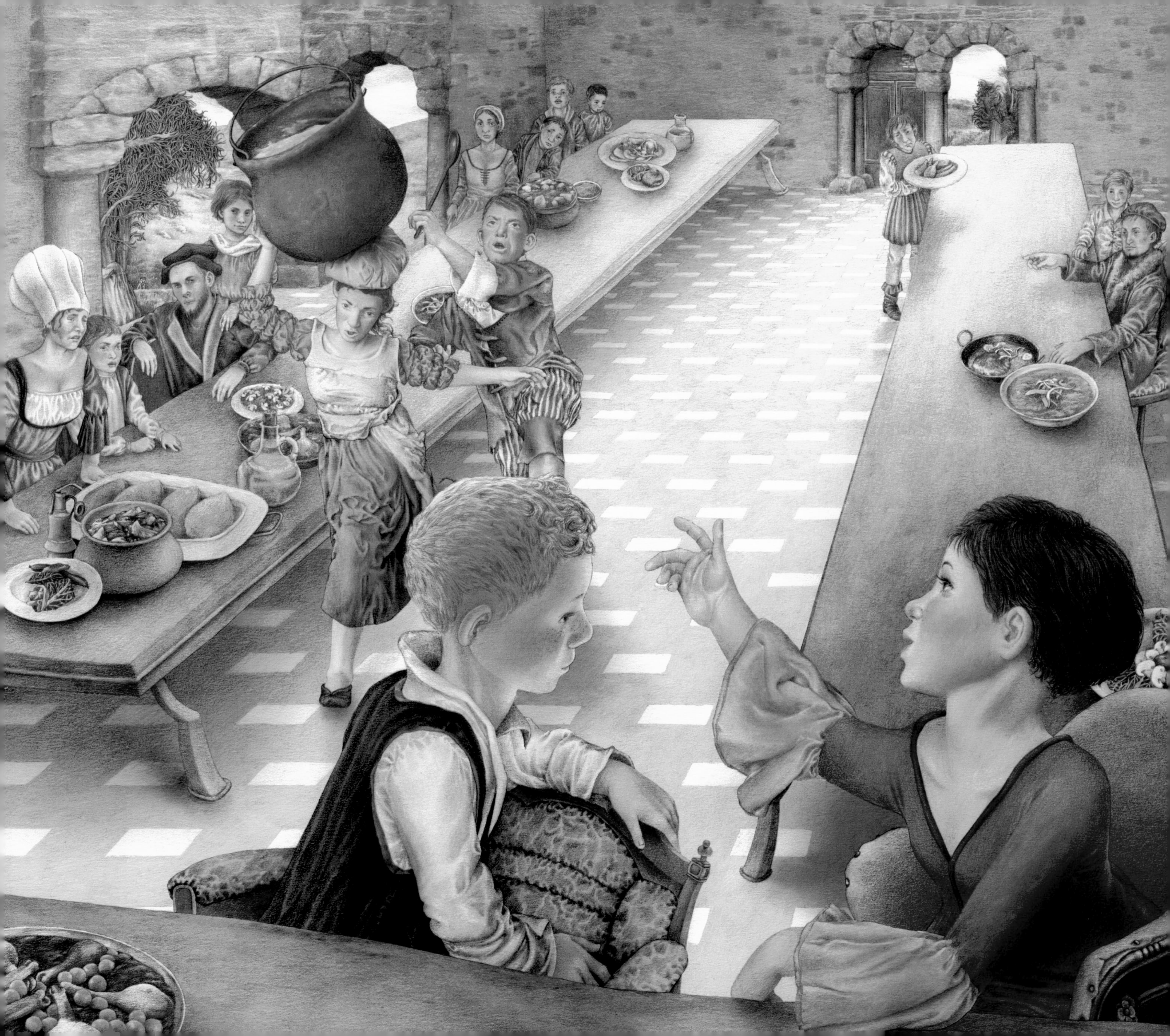

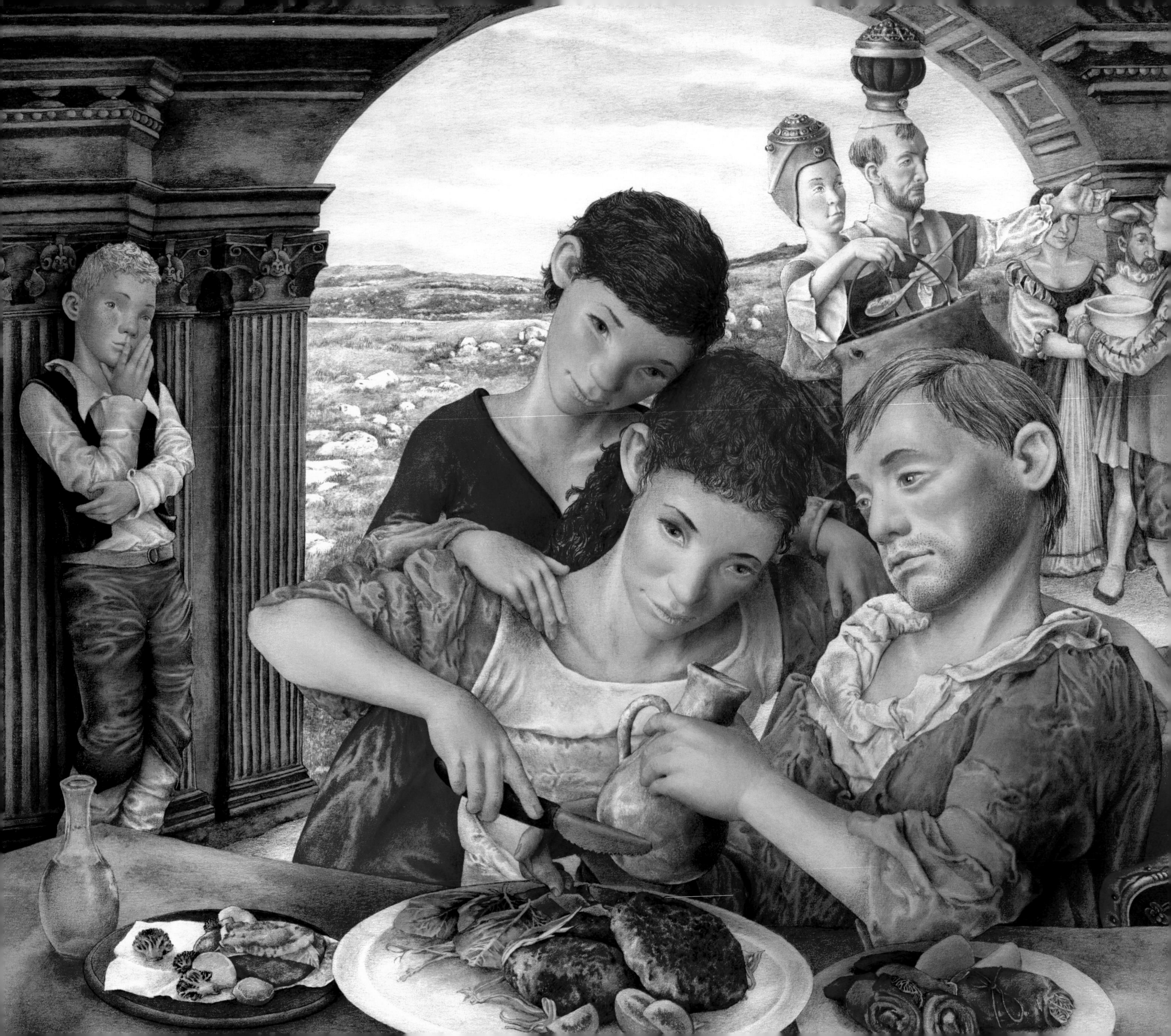

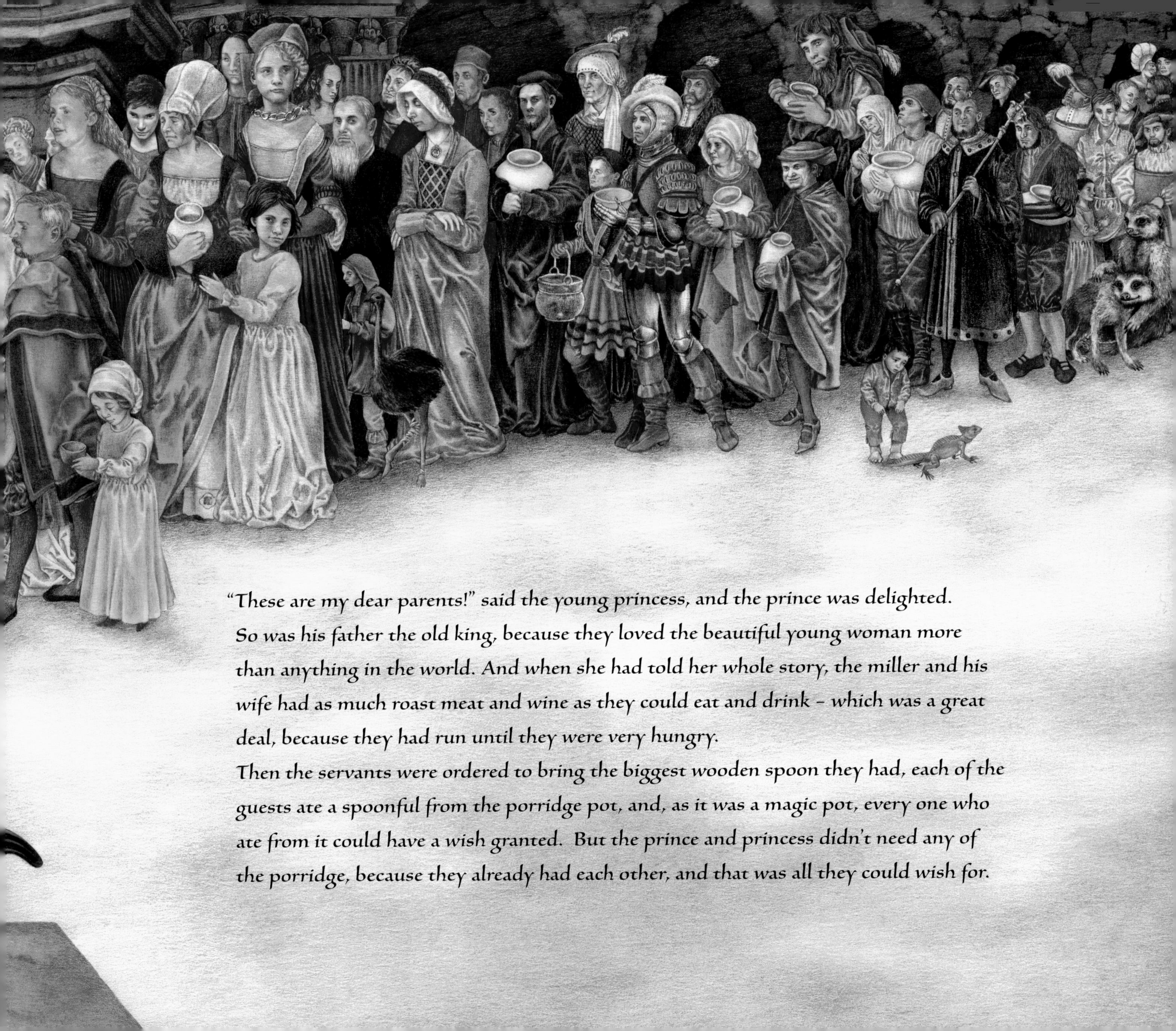

"These are my dear parents!" said the young princess, and the prince was delighted. So was his father the old king, because they loved the beautiful young woman more than anything in the world. And when she had told her whole story, the miller and his wife had as much roast meat and wine as they could eat and drink – which was a great deal, because they had run until they were very hungry.

Then the servants were ordered to bring the biggest wooden spoon they had, each of the guests ate a spoonful from the porridge pot, and, as it was a magic pot, every one who ate from it could have a wish granted. But the prince and princess didn't need any of the porridge, because they already had each other, and that was all they could wish for.

JAN   2008